FIRE FIGHTING HEROES

For as long as he could remember, Billy had wanted to be a fireman when he grew up. He loved the idea of fighting fires and keeping the citizens of LEGO® CITY safe.

One day, Billy was drawing pictures of fire engines on his bed, with his faithful dog, Flash. Flash was a very special dog – he was so clever that Billy had even taught him how to do a backflip!

Suddenly Billy's dad burst into the room. "Billy, do you remember that essay you wrote last week?" he asked excitedly.

Billy sighed. "I don't want to talk about school, Dad! You promised I could play!"

"But Billy, remember how you wrote about wanting to ride in a fire engine and fly in a helicopter?" his dad said.

"Of course," Billy said. "I'm drawing fire engines and helicopters right now!"

Billy's dad grinned like he was in on a secret joke.

"Your teacher entered your essay in a competition!" he cried happily. "And it won a prize! You're going to be the special guest at the opening of LEGO CITY's brand new fire station . . . TODAY!"

Billy stared at his dad. He couldn't believe it! "YIPPEE!" he cried, leaping off his bed and running around the house, jumping for joy. Flash was very excited too and performed his best backflip!

"Dad, what are you waiting for?" cried Billy. "Let's go!"

Not long after, Billy found himself looking up at the enormous new fire station. He gasped when he saw the hi-tech helipad, the noisy sirens and the shiny fire poles. He knew that the firefighters used those when they needed to go and save somebody as fast as they could. Then there were the big, red fire engines themselves.

"Wow!" was all Billy could say. "This is . . . "

"Amazing?" his dad suggested.

"Better than that!"

"Awesome?"

"It's both – it's amaze-some!" Billy shouted.

A crowd of people had gathered to greet Billy outside the fire station. Flash was having fun darting in and out of people's legs.

"Now, Billy," his dad said. "Remember when we took Flash to the food market and he caused all that mischief? We can't have that happening today. It's your responsibility to keep him out of trouble!"

Billy laughed, remembering how Flash had stolen a string of sausages from the butcher's stall. His dad and the butcher had chased Flash all around the city! Flash could be a very cheeky dog sometimes, but he was fast and very clever too. He'd had no problem working out how to steal those sausages from the butcher!

Next, Billy and his dad went to see Fire Chief Jones, the most famous firefighter in LEGO CITY. Chief Jones was so brave that the LEGO CITY mayor himself had presented him with a golden helmet for bravery.

Chief Jones spoke cheerfully about his brand new fire engines.

"These vehicles are top of the range. As our competition winner, we'd like to give you a special treat, Billy," he said. "Would you like to join the squad on our very first drive in the new fire engine?"

"Would I?" Billy said, jumping in the air. "This is totally amaze-some!"

Riding in the fire engine was even better than Billy had imagined. The streets of LEGO CITY whizzed by as they roared along at top speed. Flash was having the time of his life too. He hung his head out of the window and the wind blasted his ears back like a pair of flapping socks!

Billy was on the edge of his seat, but Firefighter Tim and Firefighter Trevor were very relaxed. So relaxed, in fact, that they were playing cards in the back of the truck!

"You'll get used to the speed, kid," winked Firefighter Tim, who was always cheerful.

"Or not," said Firefighter Trevor, who was always grumpy. "I still spill my drink every time the siren goes off!"

Suddenly the radio crackled into life.

"Fire Team Alpha!" squawked a voice from the radio. "Reports are coming in of a huge fire at the LEGO CITY Museum!"

"There's no time to take you and Flash back to the station," Chief Jones told Billy. "Hold on tight!"

They raced to the museum, sirens blaring. Flames surrounded the building – a sign outside read 'CLOSED FOR REPAIRS'.

"Thank goodness, there shouldn't be any citizens inside!" called the Chief, already running towards the blaze. "But the exhibits could be destroyed if we don't stop this fire!"

As they headed for the fire, a LEGO CITY firefighter motorbike and an off-road vehicle arrived as back-up. All the firefighters emerged in their uniforms, ready to rescue the museum!

Billy's heart began to race. This is what he'd been dreaming of seeing for years. The whole team was here, on their way to tackle the fire and save the day!

Firefighter Trevor and Firefighter Tim needed to get inside the museum as quickly as possible to save the exhibits. They started up their chainsaws and sliced through the locked doors.

"I'm going in!" shouted Firefighter Tim, and he dived through the gap.

"I'm going in too!" shouted Firefighter Trevor, though as usual he looked a little grumpy about it.

Outside, Chief Jones and Firefighter Alex were struggling to unwind their hose.

Chief Jones turned to Billy. "We need some extra manpower! You'll have to help us, Billy – are you up to the challenge?"

Billy's mouth went dry and he shook with nerves, but he nodded and ran to help the firefighters control the hose. The hose wriggled and twisted between them. Thinking fast, Billy jumped on top of it and pinned it to the ground!

The hose bucked and flew around but slowly Firefighter Alex managed to get it under control, and pointed the hose towards the roaring fire.

The flames whooshed up into the sky, but eventually the firefighters began to get them under control.

Firefighter Tim and Firefighter Trevor emerged from the building carrying all sorts of precious things, including an Ancient Egyptian mummy!

"Hey, Billy," Firefighter Trevor called as he raced past. "What's up with your dog?"

Billy gasped as he saw what Trevor meant. Flash was yapping and pulling at the firefighter's trousers!

"He's never normally like this," Billy protested. "He's such a clever dog!"

"Never mind – it's sort of like having a mascot," shouted Fireman Tim, as cheerful as ever.

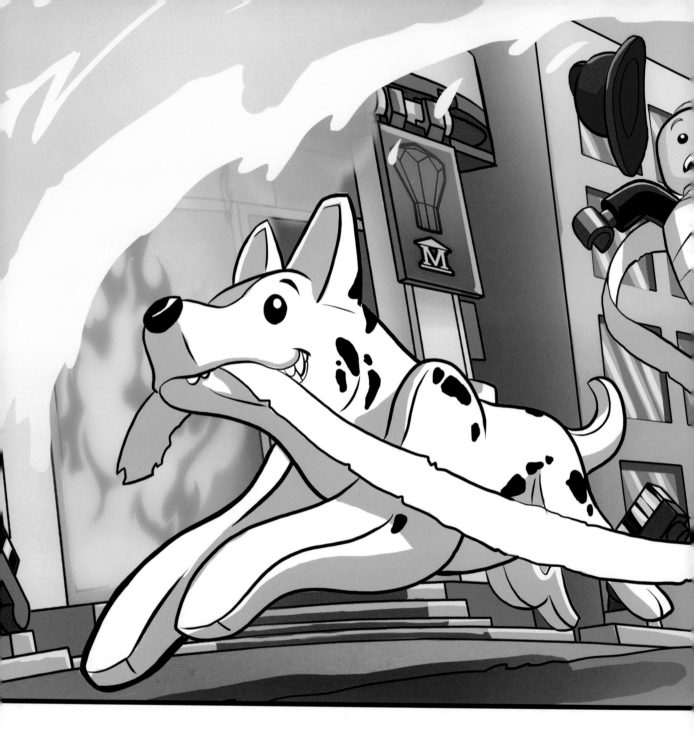

In his excitement, Flash got hold of one of the trailing bandages from the Egyptian mummy's tomb. He ran away with it like it was a string of sausages, darting in and out of the firefighters' legs until they were tangled in a web of bandages.

Firefighter Tim tripped, spinning round the ladder he was carrying . . .

Which knocked over Firefighter Alex, who was using a hose . . .
Which blasted Firefighter Albert and knocked him over!
They all tumbled down like dominoes, knocking over lots of the exhibits that
they'd rescued as they fell.

Firefighter Alex found himself hanging off a dinosaur skeleton's head. Firefighter Trevor ended up with his head stuck through a painting. And Firefighter Albert had the helmet from a Roman gladiator's suit of armour back to front on his head!

Billy was about to tell Flash off, but then he spotted that the dog's ears were perked up. Billy followed Flash's gaze towards the museum roof . . .

"Flash wasn't being naughty, he was trying to tell us something!" Billy called, pointing. "There's a second fire still going on the top floor!"

"He's right!" Chief Jones shouted. "Firefighters, aim your hose at the roof – quick!"

The firefighters all took hold of the hose, with Firefighter Tim at the front. They directed the water towards the museum roof . . . but the water pressure wasn't powerful enough to reach that high!

Billy gasped.

Chief Jones patted his shoulder. "Don't worry, Billy. The LEGO CITY firefighters always save the day . . ."

Minutes later, Billy found himself high up in the sky – in the fire department's helicopter!

It was the most thrilling thing Billy had ever done. He had written in his essay that he wanted to ride in a fire engine, use a fire hose and fly in a helicopter. And now he had ticked all three of those amazing things off his list!

The pilot flew the helicopter so it was perfectly lined up with the museum roof. "Press the blue button," Chief Jones instructed Billy. Billy did as he was told, and water jetted out of the helicopter and right into the fire.

Soon the blaze was put out. Everyone cheered. The museum was saved!

When the fire engine arrived back at the station, Billy's dad was pacing back and forth with a worried frown.

"What the blazes happened to you?" he demanded as soon as Billy arrived.

"The blazes is exactly what happened, Dad! I helped out with a real-life fire!" Chief Jones joined Billy and his dad, and gave them a big grin.

"It's true," Chief Jones said. "We couldn't have fought the fire without Billy and Flash. They're both heroes."

Billy's dad looked impressed, and he ruffled his son's hair proudly.

"You're always welcome to visit the station whenever you like," Chief Jones told Billy. "And we've got one last treat for you and Flash before you go, too."

The chief brought two gifts out from behind his back. Billy's was a shiny gold medal – and Flash's was one of his favourite dog biscuits, with a ribbon tied around it!

Flash wagged his tail so hard that it banged on the side of the fire engine like a drum.

"This time it's easy to see what he's trying to tell us!" Chief Jones said, and everyone laughed happily.

THE END